To Geni

B. A.

To my son, Anton

B. I.

∽

Text copyright © 2009 by Brian Alderson
Illustrations copyright © 2009 by Bagram Ibatoulline

First edition 2009

Library of Congress Cataloging-in-Publication Data

Alderson, Brian.
Thumbelina / Hans Christian Andersen ; retold by Brian Alderson ; illustrated by Bagram Ibatoulline.
p.   cm.
Summary: A tiny girl no bigger than a thumb is stolen by a great ugly toad and subsequently
has many adventures and makes many animal friends, before finding the perfect mate in a warm
and beautiful southern land.
ISBN 978-0-7636-2079-0
[I. Fairy tales.]   I. Ibatoulline, Bagram, ill. II. Andersen, H. C. (Hans Christian),
1805–1875. Tommelise. English. III. Title.
PZ8.A36Th 2009
[E]—dc22   2008027721

09 10 11 12 13 SCP 10 9 8 7 6 5 4 3 2

Printed in Humen, Dongguan, China

This book was typeset in Centaur.
The illustrations were done in acryl gouache and watercolor.

Candlewick Press
99 Dover Street
Somerville, Massachusetts 02144

visit us at www.candlewick.com

HANS CHRISTIAN ANDERSEN

Thumbelina

retold by BRIAN ALDERSON

illustrated by BAGRAM IBATOULLINE

CANDLEWICK PRESS

That's where it all started,
said the swallow.

That's where the woman went off
to see the local witch. She wanted a baby
real bad and thought the witch could help.
"I don't mind what sort," the woman said.
"I just want a baby."

So the witch gave her a barleycorn.
"Put it in a pretty pot, and you will see
what you will see."

There it was in the pot.
First a bud came up, all tightly folded.
Then—*pop!*—it opened out, and tucked up
inside was a baby girl, no bigger than your thumb.
So they called her Thumbelina.

Such a pretty nursery they made for her,
all cozy, there on the windowsill.

Come the spring, and who looks in at the open window
but old Mrs. Toad? *"Rek-kek-kek-kek.* What a catchi-
catchi-catch. She shall wed my Toadikins."

She carried Thumbelina out to an eddy of the river and put her on a lily pad; then she took Thumbelina's bed down to set up a home with Toadikins in the mud.

Thumbelina wept big tears, but the river fish heard what was going on, and they nibbled at the lily pad stalk and—

whisht!—away it floated down the river.

My, my, how Thumbelina laughed,
and when a butterfly joined her on her little boat,
she took off her sash and let the butterfly whiz
her along like a water-skier.

But then—oh, dear—*rrrrrh!* A great maybug came by.
"Here's a pretty thing!" he said, and he carried Thumbelina
off to the maybug tree. (Nobody knows what happened to
the poor butterfly with the sash.)

"Pooh!" said a gaggle of girlie maybugs. "Horrid! Look!
Only two legs, no feelers, a skinny little waist! Looks like
a human being." So the maybug decided that Thumbelina
wasn't so pretty after all, and he took her down and
dumped her on a daisy.

Bad times then for Thumbelina. She wandered all summer long in the forest, and when fall came and winter, she could barely keep alive.

But one day there she was at Mrs. Fieldmouse's house,
begging a crust of bread. "Oh, you poor, dear thing. Come in,
come in! Why—you can stay here and keep me company.
You can keep the place tidy and do the dishes—and every
day you can tell me a story and I'll teach you to play the flute."

Not long after, Mrs. Fieldmouse said to expect a visitor:
"A well set-up gentleman; he has his own drawing room and
a real fur coat. He'll make you a good husband, and since he
can't see to read, you can tell him stories, too."

And there he was at the door: a pompous fellow, winking and blinking, for he hated the light of day and all the world that lay above his hole.

He took them along to see his underground mansion.
Halfway there, dead on the floor, was a swallow who hadn't
been able to fly away before the winter came.

The Man in Gray poked his cane through his tunnel roof so that they could see where to tread. "What a rash and heedless fellow that is," he said. "See what happens to you when you go out up there."

Thumbelina was sad about the swallow and secretly brought along a little blanket and some mouse fur to cover the poor thing. But listen! What was that? *Burdum . . . burdum . . . burdum.* It was a heartbeat, for the swallow wasn't dead but frozen cold.

All winter long she cared for him. She didn't tell Mrs. Fieldmouse or the Man in Gray for fear that they would think her foolish, for by this time they had settled on the wedding. The Man in Gray had fallen for Thumbelina's storytelling and her music.

Spring came. The swallow was ready to fly away. "Climb on my back," he said. "Let us both go into the great forest." But Thumbelina wouldn't leave Mrs. Fieldmouse and the dishes and the storytelling. "She has been so kind to me," she said. So the swallow flew up on his own through the hole in the roof.

But the mouse was not so kind as to forget the wedding, and all through the summer she made preparations. Thumbelina had to spin the thread for her wedding dress, and four spiders were hired to weave the fabric.

"Now don't be obstropolous," said Mrs. Mouse when Thumbelina moaned about having to live underground. "Otherwise I shall bite you with my little white teeth. What a man you've got, with his fur pelisse and all those larders and drawing rooms!"

Then it was the wedding day. Thumbelina stood at the
door, bidding farewell to the world she was losing, when
suddenly: *"Chiweet, chiweet, chiweet!"*—it was the swallow.
"Winter comes," he chirruped. "Winter . . . winter . . .
winter. Let us fly together to the sun."

That's what they did. Thumbelina climbed onto the
swallow's back, and southward they flew to the swallow's
summer villa.

No toads or maybugs or old gray men there. Only the
Crystal Fairies, dwelling as Thumbelina once had dwelled,
in the buds and blossoms of the flowers.

And there she stayed and married the Crystal King,
while the swallow watched over her and brought her news
every year from the land of her birth. And it is he,
of course, who's been telling you this story.